Red Cottage

DENNIS FINNELL

The University of Massachusetts Press
AMHERST

Copyright © 1991 by Dennis Finnell
All rights reserved
Printed in the United States of America
LC 90-43308
ISBN 0-87023-667-9(cloth); 668-7(paper)

Designed by Jack Harrison
Set in Adobe Trump Medieval
Printed and bound by Thomson-Shore, Inc.

Library of Congress Cataloging-in-Publication Data
Finnell, Dennis.
   Red cottage / Dennis Finnell.
    p. cm.
   ISBN 0-87023-667-9 (alk. paper). — ISBN 0-87023-668-7 (pbk.: alk. paper)
   I. Title
PS3556.I4969R4   1991
   811' .54—dc20   90-43308
                                                          CIP

British Library Cataloguing in Publication data are available.

To Glenn Finnell
And to the memory of Margaret Finnell

Contents

The Cloud of Unknowing   1

One: Took off on time

Belladonna   5
Banzai   7
Saturday Night   8
The Grand Burlesque   10
Taking Leave of St. Louis   12
Just outside Emporia, Kansas   16
One Hundred and Fifty Springs in Hannibal   17
Europe   19
Some Reasons for Everything   20

Two: Consumed by reciprocal trade

As If to Speak   23
On the Lookout for Neighbors   24
Everybody's Business   26
Little Cloud of Dust   28
Red Cottage   29
The Isle of Lepers   30
Blue Vault   31
Over *Voice of America*   33

Three: Inside mother-of-pearl

Singing Tree   37
Made in the Shade   38
In the Stars   40

The Milk of Our Own Kind   42

The Sea Watchers   44

Swimming at Night   45

Near the Ruins of Dunstanburgh Castle   46

The Queen Bee under the Waterfall   48

White Stone   49

Four: Somewhere someone must be spinning a prayer wheel

From Attu, 1943   55

Altar Boys   57

Only Human   59

The Deposition   60

Trespassing on McKenzie Creek   62

The Fifth Season   64

The Peaceable Kingdom   67

Five: The widening V of its wake

The Sentence of Memory   71

The Great Bear over Grand Junction, Colorado   72

Bear Skull in the Attic   73

Pass It On   74

Lost Landscape   76

Third Island   78

Triptych: A Joyful Noise   80

ACKNOWLEDGMENTS

I am grateful to the editors of the following publications in which some of these poems originally appeared:

Alaska Quarterly Review: "As If to Speak"
The Agni Review: "Everybody's Business"
The Chariton Review: "Altar Boys"; "Blue Vault"; "The Isle of Lepers"; "Near the Ruins of Dunstanburgh Castle"; "One Hundred and Fifty Springs in Hannibal"; "Saturday Night"; "The Sentence of Memory"; "Trespassing on McKenzie Creek"; "Taking Leave of St. Louis"
College English: "Red Cottage"
Denver Quarterly: "Only Human"; "On the Lookout for Neighbors"; "Over Voice of America"; "Third Island"
Forum: Visual Arts/Mid-America: "The Sea Watchers — After Edward Hopper"
Intro 11: "Some Reasons for Everything"
New England Review and Bread Loaf Quarterly: "Europe"; "The Great Bear over Grand Junction, Colorado"
New Letters: "Bear Skull in the Attic"; "The Peaceable Kingdom"; "Triptych: A Joyful Noise"; "White Stone"
The New Republic: "The Cloud of Unknowing"
Poetry East: "Singing Tree"
Poetry Now: "Just outside Emporia, Kansas"
Prairie Schooner: "The Deposition"; "From Attu, 1943"; "The Queen Bee under the Waterfall"
River City: "The Fifth Season"; "Pass It On"
Sequoia: "Banzai"
Southern Poetry Review: "Made in the Shade"
Tar River Poetry: "Belladonna"

With special gratitude to David Graham, correspondent

The Cloud of Unknowing

Took off on time, and over the Gold Coast
saw Lake Michigan evaporating
in veils of fog, and the fog similarly
ascending into clouds. We're in the clouds

now, United Flight 406, and a large man is consumed
by reciprocal trade, — "Our soybeans,
their labor!" Isn't electricity
running inside others, this animal fear

alternating with awe? We are flying
inside mother-of-pearl clouds, and our iced drinks
do not tremble. Big Jim is laughing
open-mouthed, silent, to what we hope

are a comedian's words inside his headphones.
Somewhere someone must be spinning a prayer wheel,
and we fly on into a cloud, a stately
pleasure dome. "What keeps us here?" the Khan asks.

Lake Michigan flashes sunlight from its face,
and a long ore boat pulls the widening
V of its wake, floating on nothing
but water, and all of the words for water.

ONE

Took off on time

Belladonna

Apparently, my people begin and end in Iowa,
with one Mary Keenan who suddenly
showed up in Council Bluffs, ready to scrub
the prairie from their duds and oak floors.

Beyond her, the tribe exists in a fog bank,
the clouds of paradise to some,
gruel to others. They are all anonymous,
except in a general Irish way, faceless

without the luxury of portraits handed down.
They mill around, waiting to shuffle this way
as Mary has, fog parting like parlor drapes,
her carpetbag shifted from hand to hand.

Packed inside are some heartbreaking things,
I just know, from the old country.
Name them, a general nostalgia commands.
They're heavy enough, heavy enough.

What I focus on, want to heft in my
real hands, are the potatoes hidden
in her bag, bound in rags like small mummies,
the eyes beginning to sprout. For her

they mean food, hope, or a last mercy stroke:
seed potatoes for the Iowa spring,
raw ones in winter if no floors need scrubbing,
or the lethal eyes if winter fails.

Never eat the eyes, my mother told me
as she peeled spuds, skins coiling
off like party streamers. I never have,
nor downed bleach with its skull and crossbones,

played chicken, my neck on the track,
or roulette with a real pistol.
I can't say if eating the eyes of potatoes
can kill, or how our family warning began.

Maybe with Mary's last winter, the last
parlor floor in Council Bluffs cleaned,
spring just a memory of chlorophyll,
and the plain potatoes, their eyes, mercy.

There is no work here, Mary. Go back
into whatever the fog is, to faces
more real to you than any descendant's here.
However stunning your face,

the flowers of potatoes, *Solanum tuberosum*,
might kill. It's wrong conjuring you,
beautiful lady. Give us peace,
a homely thing, mostly water and edible.

Banzai

My first name, as yours, comes from a human.

Man I faced once in a censored picture
and my father's cured words, he used both hands
to keep my father on the earth in war.

Two soldiers grinning "Banzai" for the lens,
Dennis weighing his forearm on the scale
of Glenn's shoulder. "On those goddamned islands
he'd dance like Chaplin, and I'd feel alive."

Glenn's words, one photo, and Dennis escaped
back to farm the generations of calves.

Named for such men, we may as well be named
for milk, fingers, an orange sliced in half . . .

and in time on the next farm new creatures
will walk toward the plain voice calling our names.

Saturday Night

When our streetlamp blinks at the corner
a watchdog digs up his best bone,
the meanest neighbor lady
shouts her last child home with ice cream
and we start Saturday night.

Hunched over the dresser,
its glass top littered with tricks,
a woman snoops in her mirror,
spying on flaws. A crack, there,
a wrinkle, here. She believes
beauty begins with subtraction.

The man in the bathtub
soaks until Monday's greasy fingerprints
bob to the surface
and fall apart like worn-out storms.

I sit on last Sunday's newspaper,
polishing shoes with his lighter fluid,
her old nylons, and my spit.
He yells, Elbow grease!
If he can't see his face shine
in their toes I'll wash dishes
a month of Sundays.

She calls me to pluck an eyebrow.
With tweezers I yank the stubborn one
to make her perfect.
I scrub his back and shoulders
until his tattoos shine.
His back is a turtle shell,
his shoulders are coconuts.

Tomorrow, the ride in the Chrysler,
donuts after Mass, the big newspaper,
and a complete dinner.
Tonight he brings rouge to her cheeks,
she maps his hilly back.
Under their door a blessing slides
in case they rise before I wake.

The Grand Burlesque

Somewhere here the women stripped and the comics
waited for laughs. Pasties
undulated in the carnal spotlight, and baggy pants
bumped and grinded. Over the expiring

punch lines, over the houselights blacking out on cued rim shots,
The Grand Theater loomed. What was that space for
if not our communal want?
The Grand stood there and took it, the swinging pendulum,

the city's medicine ball. In the liberated air
The National Museum of Bowling solidified, ferro-concrete,
windowless. We must pay to see the renowned tools
of the masters. Where comics

joked about Wun Hung Lo,
a champion's polished ball is exhibited, under glass.
Now we can laugh, a Rip Van Winkle laugh.
There's no commercial irony here, just chronic coincidence.

Once boys presented their fevered faces to the ticket booth.
Under age, lust aged us.
We paid extra for balcony seats, for intimate
eye contact with strippers exiting stage right, flashing

their G-strings, a vision, beatific.
A dollar more for balcony, our feelings luxuriously private.
A scattering of older men below,
their faces tilted back for revelation, and empty seats

for citizens who didn't need to see. Who needs
to recollect, anyhow? Whole faces, whole bodies,
are distilled. What remains is an emotional hangover.
The combo in the orchestra pit,

for example, as good as dead.
But the sax man's feigned indifferent tone, as though
desire were ennui, that's the pitch we take across the river,
and the drummer's tardy pedalwork, the piano player's

progression of three blue chords. From balcony seats
we spied the comic in the wings.
His name, Muckin' Fuch; his plight, to stare at each stripper,
seeing each embodied verdict, every naked "no."

And what did we see in "The Dance of the Lover's Hands"?
Her hands were our hands, her orchestrated moaning
coming from the staged memory
of the watcher's flesh, from the pretense of hands.

A drum roll, a rim shot, and the houselights black out.
For nothing we will let you feel the lace netting
over her bed, the gauze between skin and voyeur,
between boys and a hard place.

Taking Leave of St. Louis

Nota: man is the intelligence of his soil,
The sovereign ghost. . . .
Nota: his soil is man's intelligence.
That's better. That's worth crossing seas to find.
—WALLACE STEVENS

1.

Smoke used to rise in any shape we wanted,
llama, mountain, neighbor girl, even the sleeping
face of a grandfather. We felt kites pull,
but little how smoke took refuge up there,
suburb of clouds. It falls over our homecoming,
odor calling up a factory at blank heat,
red bandana and neck, a man's pupils, pinpricks.

If it had color, this odor would be the brown
vein of the Mississippi. Just a breath or two
drives sorrow to our feet. The few remaining
tenement homes, spray-painted confessions
down front stoops, tiny yards where dust rises
up as funnels the size of children, these will not
walk away. And Spring? It's a curse to alley weeds.

Cousin, show your heart, from the same orchard
as mine. Let's plan to forget these windows
boarded pitifully up and look ahead
where we're driving. The bridge's legs built
stone on bedrock hold us up out of grace,
don't they? And the spans arching us prove
people did, and we must, alter our stories,

so gaze as far into water the shade of our city
as the river allows. What inches under us
with a prehistoric moan if the ear is turned right
is no patriarch. It lies there, the weary giant
offspring of rain and of mud giving way.
This bridge feeds us to the metal arch curving

pain into understanding. James, people made
this rainbow, even the elevator rocking us
inside its leg, and the room at the top shaped
as cut onyx where it's hard to walk, and downturned
windows where our faces are meant to show.

The Old Cathedral: a toy of distance.
A high-rise window is rectangled sunlight.
Something is forgotten there. Bad relations?
In the middle of the city a man is falling.

2.

Once, I did live near orchards, peach and
apple and pear. I drove gravel
roads alone spring nights bordered by
trees laid out in grids. The orchard keepers'

clapboard houses sat stories above the bowed
limbs, and like ether
light went out their windows onto the arching
flowered limbs, seeped inside them,

then gone. How they got there I pictured as
immigration, clans speaking a cross of old
and new tongues and walking oxen under loads
over the Sawatch, down Debeque Canyon

to there, the valley opening as old words,
kept. Oxen pulled to lather
wagonloads of saplings readied to go into
their quincunx, roots bound in burlapped

globes of the old dirt, the finger-size
trunks of peach and pear and apple tagged
Prunus persica, or *Pyrus,* both
communis and *malus.* Wise and faithless

as a beast I drove orchards, white moths
hectic in my headlights from tree
to blossoming tree. Whose winters but mine
coerced me to see moths as parts of flowers,

migrating orchard to orchard in the common
will to be fruitful. I would halt
between two orchards, switch engine and lights
off to let trees and moths back inside

their darkness. And to let me picture

myself as cave salamander, eyes withered
to nubs, organs visible past
transparent flesh, who with touch alone
must know where the world ends, I begin.

3.

A man is falling in the middle of the city.
It might be bad to say once more that he stretches
his limbs in air, has a yawn on his face.
Bad as a child who won't let the thing alone.

His eyes, wide open now, are taking in the earth
below him, and us, too easy to forget.
Gravity is not love. His eyes, bluish, the pupils
constricted black into which stars and nothing go.

I'm tired of cause and effect. James, let us
retell his story, one like an arch, a bridge
growing out of pain to justice. Pears withered.
He walked absent-mindedly out the window.

And I want to walk off as refugee, with a tidy
bundle of goods balanced on my head.
Then he never will fall as the newspapers said.
The right sound makes the possible necessary?

You may be right, cousin. As he falls his sleeves
ruffle in the wind he makes. Are witnesses
accomplices?
                    Or else he stays

rooted in air, a tree in the sky, untethered kite,
a blanched face. If you call him your uncle
he must come down, and we must drive through a city
as through a being that was once our body.

Just outside Emporia, Kansas

Air thickens from the smell of burnt hair
and cowshit and the sweetness,
nearly edible, of freshly cut alfalfa.
Just outside Emporia, Kansas,

thirty-two cattle trucks are huddled,
driverless, against the corrugated walls
of the Iowa Meat Packers Plant.
Diesel engines idle like dozing animals.

Between the red slats of trailers
only the large, yellowed eyes of cows
or tails switching away horseflies.
Over the galvanized slaughterhouse roof,

heat is strung up.
Just outside Emporia, Kansas,
Coronado discovered Quivera at last,
hidden under a mound of buffalo bones.

He ate the tongue of a servant's horse
and ordered the tail woven into rope.
My father rode through town at night,
clinging to the belly of a boxcar,

praying to stop, hands locked together
around an axle. His pantleg smoldered
from rail sparks, and singed hair
did not grow back. A five-pointed star

brands his thigh where fire died out.
Just outside Emporia, Kansas, an empty
cattle truck passes me on a downgrade,
and I taste fumes for miles past Piedmont.

One Hundred and Fifty Springs in Hannibal

That Spring the teenagers filled the sandbags,
as was the custom, then built the levee
as tall as their shoulders. Mothers raised
their babies overhead for a first look,
and said *River* and said *Wall of Sand*.

The flagpole sitter kept his winter promise,
one day in a shack on a tower
for each town year. He grew a civil beard,
squeezed out a waltz on a concertina.
Fathers in parlors cultivated the old tongues.

The river, he would not rise. Dogs whelped
from our husbandry, irises flourished.
The flood that we built the wall to survive
showed up downriver in the Bootheel.
And we, the townspeople, walked the dry levee,

the band playing dance tunes in the square,
two or three of us touching the wall
as mourners, to forgive, put their fingers
into names in stone, a woman in a bonnet
handing out red poppies, free and real.

That April the chills came over the old man —
a Mr. Taylor — downstairs. He tapped
his ceiling with a broom handle
Send down some heat. He blamed the river,
he blamed me, as though my winters were in him.

And that May a woman brushed out the blonde
tint in her hair. She sat at her dresser,
mean to herself, working the brown
roots out, speaking of her alias, her eyes
blacked out in photos, the platinum bouffant.

The flagpole sitter climbed down in June.
As the flood we needed failed
the town went into its history at last.
The Gulf of Mexico took in our years.
New dogs napped on porches in a first July.

Summer came in cicadas. My bride watched
a neighbor shoulder a catfish up
the alley of smells and silence. It had jaws
to take young turtles, birds tired of flight,
eggs dropped from the bridge by a boy.

Europe

What must be Holsteins amble down to the beach,
gazing past the belittled oil tanker
toward the Netherlands. Old ones lie down,
resting near clumps of sea oats, delicate legs

folded beneath their tender undersides.
Younger ones stand, domestic as sawhorses,
unamazed that ribs do not puncture
black-and-white skins. They look to the land

where reason bred them and where a lonely god,
fleshed out as a chestnut bull,
tricked a beautiful maiden into bearing us.
They gaze; they ponder another whole day

meant for grazing. For hours they must chew
essential pain until two hands
draw milk out of their bodies into wooden pails
or until their teats are hooked up

to machines. One of them moans. She will not
stop bellowing. Maybe her udders, full,
hurt her. Her moans must die at sea in the white
momentary tangle of blue sky, bluer water.

Like that woman who mothered a continent, she knows
ideal pain suckling her masters,
baby gods she must nurse, must die before.
She totters to her feet; bows her head;

bellows across faceted seas to the Low Countries.
After her, silence lasts one breath;
then the sea, like an engine, rumbles into being.
In her lowing animals live on and on.

Some Reasons for Everything

She cuts the eyes from potatoes
and feeds bucketfuls to the pigs.
He cleans out old mattresses
and stuffs them with fresh cotton.
She brushes the sorrel mare named May.
He climbs between the wheels of the boxcar.
Their gestures shape the air
between them into something else.
She gathers warm eggs in her skirt.
He spades up dark red beets.

Where they are the sky comes down
to their feet and onto their backs.
They shuffle along, kicking up dust,
and feel the sky between their fingers.
Between them are numbers of miles,
several counties, a few towns,
and the three-headed god
of seeds, of soil, of chance.
With their hands they pat the air
into the notion of a child.

Because she believes in God
I will sneeze three times on Tuesday.
Because he picks his teeth with a matchstick
I will believe in God.
Her tying a ribbon in my sister's hair
will persuade me love is needed.
His weeping at the kitchen table
will give me bitter encouragement.
Because they shared a blackened room
for a split second and loved
one another with their bodies,
my first word was *light*.

TWO

Consumed by reciprocal trade

As If to Speak

What became of the old woman at the window
can trouble words a long time,
and who her broach went to, as well as
the flowered dress she mercilessly tugged at.

Maybe it is just to give her a sister,
younger, ashamed, and once pretty who is seen
as one bare arm, white and strong,
pulling her back from sight.

Up the street my shoes echoed off stone walls.
She tapped twice, then three times, at her window,
moving lips as if to speak.
I thought the glass pane shook in its frame,

as if to speak. Woman in the window,
noises vibrate the littlest bones
in their white begging bowl.
You there, help me with these windows.

On the Lookout for Neighbors

We, the feeble, sit alone on the lookout for winter.
Our best windows clouded with breath, our wills
dormant as snails, is it not hard labor recalling
leaves jostled in the sycamore? "O daddy not
that again," my daughter might say if I had one.

If I had one I would tell her, But it's January!
The sycamore is again an old self, a stick of a god
aborigines drew in their cavern. The bark peels
back in the white of baby teeth. Child in me says
bootprints in snow circling the tree are my neighbors'.

It says a mother and daughter trudged out in snow,
just because. The daughter did make believe
the sycamore was the statue of the lady you climb in,
saying the right words. And the mother? She did
neigh and stomp in snow as the pony for her daughter,

all a bad lie. No daughter waved from a make-believe
statue's crown, and no mother neighed on all fours in snow.
Two boys left the prints in snow. Out my window I
watched them circle the sycamore, firing silent and new
air rifles into an old nest, finding no sparrows.

Father, where are our neighbors if not with the tree?
I can't say, Amelia. All we hear beyond our wall
is the ocean that talks in the shell, that static
from the ones who disappeared. No single voice from
mother or daughter sets our littlest bones to quiver.

Our neighbors, gone. Long ago in distance and black
good stories make up, a star left her six sisters,
overworked father, mother pretty as clouds. Why,
father? Some say family troubles, her electric charm.
Now we see it as we must. I would not picture it.

Everybody's Business

A moth called their window into being.

It spread day-old wings and pressed the shriveled
grub of its body against the pane,
holding what had passed for air in place.

Their windows could have housed dressed manikins.
Life-sized panes faced the little courtyard,
hardly a courtyard, of trash bins, an iron table,
one chair. Night came an hour earlier there;
day, in metallic clamor followed by whiffs
of yesterday's stew, arrived before real dawn.

It was a night after a day like any other.
They sat, and sit, with rigid backs offered
as souvenirs, heads bowed in the vain act
of eating. Silverware is clinking, never to be
crossed on plates. Grains of salt are falling

that man and that woman will not let fall.
They shy away from memory. Sure, his sideburn
is curly and her chin nondescript, but bona fide
legs are missing. Maybe windows compromise us,
fingers of intimacy framed to look public.
Glass is solid. Beneath the windowsill
is more her weakness needs him to admire.

It's lethal seeing through things. Air is mortal,
the moth may suffer, windows can melt back
to histories. Facts can do those people in.
It's not enough to say *ear* and *chin*, *elbow* and *hand*.
When the story is good, salt falls on its own,
a cheek rises, and a forearm twists in its skin.

The dead remain dead. Everybody else must go on
thinking up biographies. Those two draw curtains
for the night to take hold so the four-legged ones
can make their courtyard rounds. Andrew rubs shyness
out of her back, the fear of immortality,
her backbone a snake, Marie, shedding white skin.

Little Cloud of Dust

So many really interesting professions
now open to us, from soup to nuts, from game theory
to grace analysis. In the get-up of childhood
you shot a pigeon, testing the tenderness in the feathered
world, whether a Casper-like ghost with wings
would steam up, and how many BBs would make you wise.
Some of us scrambled ants in a skillet, young
Mr. Wizard's tasting iron and piss,
sprinkling the skeletons in roses for bees.

Today I'm the nirvana for eggs
and carry around like in a money belt an old game.
Walk in the dirt, a stone to your eye, investing
the dust with a miniature city, with people too small
to play house with. Watch the stone fall
through the imagined stratosphere, until it kicks up
a little cloud of dust. Your target blown to smithereens,
it's a milk run. Missed, and you're shot down
again, a smoking comet, and you die, a little.

Was this my game, my genius, or something in the air?
Men inside a mountain wear it around
their mature waists. Old playmates of ours, shot down over
dirt and make-believe cities, they rose up
to see a toy world mapped in light on screens,
and to listen for an empire's thundering horses.

Red Cottage

You know how it is.
Your accident lets you meet a long-lost friend,
one whose love meant the world to you.
What's coincidence
but a slender awareness of merged parallels,
a thing you suspect goes on all the time.
Harmony, a kiss, a word you savor on your tongue,
all striving toward the horizon,
toward that depot.

Well, imagine how I feel.
Tolstoy died in a red cottage.
I am renting a red cottage!
Now I occasionally look toward the snowy woods
for Sophia wringing her hands,
that woman held at arm's length from her husband, dying.
But all this is bullshit.
I live in a red cottage
between a ridge named after an eager animal,
and a river called by some Breath of the North.

Wouldn't you feel once in a while
that what surrounds you
is the makings for a folktale,
a legend, a story to bring children up by,
then doubt as they grow body hair, their voices changing?
And so I feel haloed by this stammering white air,
blizzard, the black shawled mourners in the woods
nothing more than hungry wild fowl,
and a hateful man dead who put blood and bread together.

The Isle of Lepers

Once more someone has set fire to the foothills,
little mountains of scrub pine, of Fords
shuttled up dry creekbeds and left for better
or worse. Once more a long island of smoke

waits overhead. I can call it The Isle of Lepers,
then simply look back down. No, island,
you did not come from seasoned leaves and a boy
who helped them on to air and ashes. Now

some things this March are unwilling to burn.
Here in Tennessee I know some poor white
is to blame for smoke, for me naming it The Isle
of Lepers and for naming him Jody, The Redneck.

My sky in sickness draws out my own sick wisdom—
The one called Jody kneels. With his thumbnail
he strikes a wood match. Now a pine goes up.
I make him trudge the dry creek, leaving his Ford.

Once more someone has set fire to the foothills,
contorted limbs of redbud, cars abandoned
after joy rides, a tortoise bearing a burden,
creatures from the three worlds. Their new selves

spiral up to the island of smoke. I am alone.
Down here I am left to look up to the island
home for ones of fear, to try to forget Jody,
the one I thought up and who thought up the island.

Down here the young man I was will not forget me
in the poverty of fear, burning letters that shamed
one of two lovers, my lightning war, mine,
words going to smoke and dirt, words expiring.

Blue Vault
— *for William Hoagland*

I think of you today and make you sad.
Out of friendship you swallow Sanka
tan with milk in a state that Spaniard
named for mountain. He chiseled the year
fingernail deep into the cottonwood burned
for immigrant warmth. His word, *Montana*,
stands by your roads in place of Cibola.

Look my way and imagine
what your eyes cannot take in.
Like mind, breath is a sack for the world
keeping it as we'd know it. The yolk
is whole in albumen, the fetus floats
in its bag of brine. If I see your eyes,
their gray pupils dilated out of need,
unable to take in this mountain and that,

maybe it's because I envy faithfulness
shepherding you to the plains that you
have a right to. I make your gestures
semi-final, handsome. Get up from your desk;
light a good cigar; gaze south for those Rockies,
these Smokies, mountains that can unite us.
Say something about distance and air
bluing the common snow we believed white.

There is not a thing wrong with the sky
colored by sight and words. Out of friendship
I walk Havre, Montana, with the sadness
we need to imagine, stopping on the bridge

*painted silver over Milk River running tan.
Frowning with necessity, I think of you,
rememberer and remembered one, as you light
a cigarette in Tennessee and turn to look
out toward me, naming a feeling for us.*

Over *Voice of America*

Some nights the quiet is all wrong. A tape,
it plays white noise. These nights I crown
myself in earphones and tune the short-wave in
to new music of the sphere. Grandmother voice
over Radio Albania wants to send over a hit
about wheat, and love. Over *Voice of America*
our voice is simply enunciated as if only
foreigners have ears. Silence is a drawn chord.
Between Tirane and Washington the static is
a Geiger counter gone sane. I tune the BBC.
The Repulsive Aliens play their catchy music —
codas from the white dwarf before collapse.

Some evenings I haunt my office. Windows open
out to Mary Lyon's grave and campus maples
kept pretty by will. The hour we love between
dog and wolf comes as stars show up, up there
all along. In my dark office I drink coffee
I cannot see, start to disappear. I make up
faces for students blasting maples and her grave
with Culture Club, The Police. Hair is green,
cheeks flour white. Mary Lyon said, "Testify!"
Dickinson took a carriage over the Holyoke Range
to her own seminary of despair, a dress
kept white in legend and a whiter sustenance.

More white than crystals Parker melted in spoons,
a hero addicted to pain. Students here know
Stalin's white Siberia and each red cent doctors
earn in their cures. They know Reggie Jackson,
Patton. Bird is black, fiendish, jazz-like.
Modifiers are right and wrong. Bird did burn
his room in a colored L.A. hotel, yelled Fire,
colored and naked. He did die in a baroness's

Manhattan suite, laughing at Dorsey on T.V.
Don't those stories kill? From L.A. to New York,
from fire to laughter, he played hopeless rooms
we can inhabit because he did not need hope.

Bird lived, died, lives some more. The last time
I visited Dickinson's grave, it was occupied.
Inside the black iron fence young lovers lay
clothed on her grave. He was on her and on her.
I have not yet been back. Friends, make sense
of those lovers. Were they mocking the virgin
in legend, she who knew Babylon inside out?
Tell me in some nights a Parker solo hums
also out of you, or a Dickinson phrase
moves your lips, cryptically. Our ears record
sounds of dead stars. Tell me we call them back
since they call us and we can hear, once again.

THREE

Inside mother-of-pearl

Singing Tree

When all your flaws become a point of view,
when your limitations let you hold what's out there
in your palms and get to know it well,
when nothing can improve the sky with its mountain ranges,
castles along a river bluff, and the sound of a bronze celesta

then maybe you'll walk out dumb one day
under a blossoming tree, who at an old distance, —
from your window, say, smudged with winter fingerprints, —
looked yellow-green and almost sick
with Spring, and see, hear, and smell a queen

who again must pass out the petals of her largesse,
tiny as the eyelids of sparrows,
and who suckles at her hundred breasts
creatures who moan, chant, and then fly off
to a city where their sweetness is bartered for a song.

Made in the Shade

Don't budge an inch, desire whispered, and I heard.
I was a willow sapling, a backyard game
after spading for the mole and the absurd

BBs I gunned at the sky. I wanted the fame
of being shot by the blue. A lead pellet
shook a green thing, and the mole of my dreams

clawed down to the asylum for blind vermin.
As for that other game, not a house sparrow
perched on my branch, nobody had it made in

my shade. Didn't you ever want to suck marrow
for being a good dog, since you love dogs?
To be touched by your master? To be Fido?

I wanted to be this willow, and take smog
in off the streets, making it sugar and air,
to be a vision for humans, as their eggs

fried and they squinted and said, *It's still there.*
But I remained a boy, and not only that,
I thought I was going blind, a stupid fur

gloving my hand at arm's length, and beyond it
my backyard a victim of generality,
a coloring book spray-painted by a mean shit.

This was a lesson, all right. Just try to see
the leaf for the tree, the bird for the sky's
blue forest. So what could I do, anyway,

but bring face to face with my nearsighted eyes
the vague ones in the exile of distance,
my hand, an oak leaf, a fallen nest the size

of two hands, cupped. No longer blurred aliens,
they came bearing gifts, their details and proud
flesh, warts and all, natural citizens,

while beyond them loitered the nations of cloud,
drooping trees in the sky, weeds in the heart,
needing the longest eye, my short eyes closed.

In the Stars

Last night and tonight I've kept an eye out
for the half-dozen stars you named
The Hurt Woman. In the house shadow
tossed by the streetlamp I've tried to stand
unmoving as one of those stones circling
the field on the island. But you know,
the head starts to soon tremble, angled up
at the salt-flecked continent between
one star-bear and a hero. And it's hard to see
past the civil lights of streetlamps guarding
our domiciles and the flimsy matches
struck for a smoke with a nightcap.
They go up and fuse in a corona
over the city, and they water down
the constellations I don't know on sight.

Know what I think? If The Hurt Woman is
up there healing in the black sanitorium,
you drew lines to six stars and jotted up
a woman from the stolid lights.
Don't get me wrong: you're no god,
unless children pencilling in their bestiaries
dot to dot are gods. In your eyes
she was the wounded one borne on a litter
down the black mountain, the hungry stars
the old ones saw as beasts kept at bay.

In my eyes another hurt woman does not heal,
pale thing, nebula, embryonic light
the ancients named ether. If I were sleepwalking
she'd be beckoning me with salt hands,
Save me, save me, down the echoing corridor
at the end of touch. *I'm just a freak,*

she'd confess, *a freak*, and she did not heal.
Our boss found her, her room tidy as
Ptolemy's sky, the ceiling resting on her eyes.

Where is your sky and where The Hurt Woman?
Not over our heads, not in the stars
pinning the suffering ones to a black vault.
Your sky is interior, a nervous system,
and The Hurt Woman must be burning you
as she heals in the justice of a new sky.

The Milk of Our Own Kind

When sleep won't take me
and I'm working the graveyard shift of worry
I leave the bed of the one I love
for even she can't rock me to Morpheus.

Because only sweet milk can help
I touch my way to the Frigidaire and feel
like the burglar who knows
the valuables are kept in the cold.

I take my medicine from the carton
with the orange faces of missing children
and as milk goes back to a mammal
I drink something of Rosanna's or Karl's.

When I was a child with a weight problem
I knew no stranger would steal me
and uncles who could not lift me
gave me Dutch rubs in the name of our blood.

That child mailed away boxtops
at a post office with a gallery of criminals
and got back a tin star
instead of the face of the most-wanted.

Now the faces of missing children
on silver screens warn the lovers of movies
and on grocery sacks tell the hungry
of children wanted for crimes of disappearance.

Because a witness might recall my face
as the last one a child saw
I only talk to strange children
here in the dark when sleep won't take me.

I drink the milk of Rosanna and Karl
to put the bogeyman to sleep
knowing I don't make them vanish
and only our own kind will steal us.

The Sea Watchers
—*after Edward Hopper*

This couple sit on a wooden bench, their backs
to the white facade of a rented cottage, human shadows
elongated on the wall, soon to be
lost in the larger umbra. They give their gaze to the sea,

their profiles to us, faces wearing the white masks
of sunlight coming head-on. Oblivion
isn't the word, yet they don't hear the white
and red and yellow towels flapping in the sea breeze, like flags

on a vessel signaling all is well. They are mindless
of their hands curling under, gripping
invisible objects, that shape between peace and fist
we've seen before in the hands of passengers

as the airplane shudders, lifting off. They've journeyed
to inhabit rooms by the sea, from the gerrymandered
light of a city. Inside a civil animal
they left a bulb burning, fleeing, not looking back.

And even though, after swimming, skin is running
hot and cold, what with gooseflesh
and sunburn, they face the sun until it unamazingly sinks
again without a hiss, until watching so well

they no longer need to see. Before we know it
there is nothing to do but sleep,
their chests rising and falling all night long,
and the sea is the sea again, only darker.

— *for Anita*

Swimming at Night

The water is still and warm. A stillness
that my weakness calls peace, a warmth
the old human in me says is mammalian,
still harboring salt. If I step into this,
wavelets will break off from me as my name does,
paged out in the air terminal. Like the static
of the first explosion that is doing in
the everlasting. The little stars are twinkling.
The sun for months has borne down. It alone
has cracked the clay about the pool's border.
It has heated up what I think the dirt desires,
water. Miraculous kudzu and young cedars
just outside the redwood-stained fence are coming
this way, toward the pool where only the benign
outlasts the maintenance man and algaecide.
It is a summer night, air full of exhalations,
and warm and the water warmer. No one tonight
will sense me floating naked and blue
from the water lit up and colored by the one
underwater lamp and the pool's blue walls.
What flourishes outside my body? In darkness
all distance is the same. The kudzu out there
is as close as my clothes prostrate on concrete
over there, as close as the snapshot of himself
the visitor buried in the powder of the moon,
coming and going in peace. In a pool shaped
as some vital organ, some mammoth's or one
pulled out of a forsaken constellation, I float
in the heat of the mammal and lose touch
in complete touch. I will float on my back
a few minutes, watching the dark space inside Orion,
feeling pity for nothing, neither clay
nor desire, for I am warm, in love and lethal,
accomplice in the night and the stars' witness.

Near the Ruins of Dunstanburgh Castle

Just as you had pictured, sea and sky opened
the way a shell must. You stepped
just like that inside it, hitching up
a black curtain of skirt. Water, taking on
colors of sky, then sand, rose above the girlhood
scars marking your knees, and lapped there.
Your legs ended in ovals.
The rest of you stood up on its own.

Memory is loss. Thinking of you there
I get a phantom sensation, a tingling
in the air, in the here-and-now without you.
This room is hushed as the place of our forbears.

Stones that made up a castle were inching seaward.
We ignored them. We looked into
the bit of sea cupped in your hands and thought
your skin already remembered. Water
discolored your skin and magnified the broken lines
marking your palms larger than one life.
And your legs? Your legs I recall
in water blown out of daily proportion.

It all comes back. Our offspring will gaze
our room's blank walls and remember
the innocent sky needing us and think back
to the sea as our accomplice in loss.

You dragged your legs from water. They were
mottled white and pink, covered in gooseflesh.
Which of us said tomorrow is rocked
between sun and moon, that it breaches abstract

white, then corpuscular, then sounds deep
where the sea plus the whale means blackness?

It is then as now. You, me, and out there
need one another, so we walk this beaten sand
as our ancestors and our unborn walk,
forever mortal, into remembered water where
your legs are yours and are the North Sea's.

The Queen Bee under the Waterfall

Forgive me for using your Irish linen tablecloth
to remember a waterfall you did not
and will not see which granite and the water's
weight broke into shawls of lace.

Down through the purgatories of rhododendron
and past the obsessed bees I hiked
to find once more the white force that sings out
all our days. It was beautiful, the way
a Greek woman going into hell is beautiful.
It was named The Second Falls. I did not
think of you at all as I splashed
water the color of copper on my face and heard
that blank noise, hammer, anvil, and stirrup
quivering in our ears. Beauty draws us easily in
in a great breath and forges us,
beautiful too.

A bee lumbered across stones
toward the falls. She must have once been a queen.
I pictured her not at all for months, not her
abdomen slender from disuse, not her eyes
multiplying the loom of the falls,
not her memory of the hive, until I held
this yellowed cloth, memento vitae, hearing
the aria of your voice, water against stone.

White Stone
— *for Glenna Purcell*

Driving home up Five-Mile Hill could trouble
a traveler's dreams tonight, the road's
shoulder of asphalt gone ragged from two days
of April rain, danger signs on all fours
gelling in the clouds like the light-stunned deer,
their message a law for travel: to forget
is lethal. The car radio's long medley
of hits by Elvis is stopped by a bulletin —

April rains cultivate the flood of the decade,
roads memorized like hallways by touch
descending into the sudden lakes, and bridges
borne off by streams with handsome names.
So we keep in mind the hazards of travel.
That rain might foster a nothing of a gorge
to fatten itself on the road. That a glance
for mirrored headlights (another traveler

trusting me, a stranger, to tunnel through
the cloudbank) might pull us both into
the hill's lode or the hungry ditch.
So I picture the faithful world out there
that carlights cannot give whole to the eyes,
the hill's coal bulk and the mouth
of space and there solidifying in the fog,
a white stone at the roadside. I know,

this is just a road, but a white stone
calls a woman back outlasting the rain,
its work in time perfecting the lesser stones
into handfuls of sand. It calls her back,

crouched over the spaded black dirt of a new
garden, her sandals left on the grass,
a white housecoat taking in the frail light
and hovering, a kind of moon for the seedbed.

Tonight she haunts a road into fog and rain.
There is no moon, and Elvis is singing
inside the glowing radio in that tremolo of his.
He's down at the end of Lonely Street at
Heartbreak Hotel. If I could I'd interrupt
the King's ballad and send bulletins
in her voice over the air: "Watch out for bodies
cultivating the flood of desire, and shoulders

gone soft in the storm. Watch out for a drenched
stranger thumbing his way to Kingdom Come.
Keep an eye on brooks with attractive names.
Remember: curves are beautifully deadly.
Just watch out." And I would be wrong as this rain.
The King is dead. I can't put bulletins
in her mouth about desire. Then picture this —
hand-lettered signs tacked to fenceposts

along a black, Kansas highway, the two
of us peering out the window and in a duet
singing out the words we knew by heart
were waiting up the road. The Lord's Prayer
ended with Amen in a confusion of milkweed,
rusting barbed wire. Here the neon sign for Food
brands the fog red, and if I didn't know better,
the town hall in clouds would be a tug dead

in the water. Since forgetfulness is a long swim
in the river Lethe, I let up on the gas,
hearing a music box pick a waltz, the boys'
school rings inside made smaller for her with wax.
A white stone? She lies at sixteen in the bed
of near-miscarriage, the color in her face
gone to eggshell, and her mother's sheets
charted as a map of multiple desires.

FOUR

Somewhere

someone must be

spinning

a prayer wheel

From Attu, 1943

From the troopship I watched your headscarf
grow indistinct, sparrow in a willow,
feather in a nation. Past the black fjords
I was kept below waterline in a hammock,
rocking, freckled arms waking me to my hand.
The photo out of sight in my duffel,
I tossed rations to gulls skimming our wake.

At Dutch Harbor ravens guarded the hill.
Aleuts in exile from Kiska and Attu
starved aboriginal skin over Russian bones.
Under the garlic stalk of the steeple
they sit for the ikon to weep this century.
They lie three deep in the hill.

Fog kept our eyes poor. The sea was a chart
the captain touched and the ship inched.
Out there in island caves the mummies hung,
woven grass for viscera, whalebone labrets.
On Adak we built an airstrip of beach gravel.

On Kiska we filled our boys' bomb craters.
On Kiska the native tongue's clack was
Aleutian primer. Speech is whittled bone
to puncture fog to praise brother seal.

Margaret, on Attu I walk a mountain's torso.
Colossal legs must stand leagues below
where the blind crabs inch. Clouds and fog
deface a summit of raven and stone cairn.
And me? I walk across this being and speak
the giant's monologue. Michael the Aleut

carried his wife's body like a sack of rare
driftwood three days on his back. Then?
A wreath of puffin feathers. His oiled body
wrapped in sealskin, two stones for weight.
He swam with her past this to paradise
where light is the light a voice must make.

Altar Boys

St. Gregory the Great's peeling white spire
is a snapshot, now, leafed in
the organist's hymnbook to save the old
house of worship. Two decades ago

and more I paced off the miracle distance
between communion rail and the wooden
pews for the meek, waiting. And was paid
two crisp ones and worldly months

in absolution to don the black and white,
light the dark cakes of incense,
and walk around the heavier-than-human caskets,
keeping the living from the dead.

How much will you pay me to forget
the heft of black cassock, the starched
white surplice, the weight of
a boy's vestments and a gilded censer?

A penny? A penny for each of memory's
unblinking eyes to pay the limping
ferryman to pole me across the smoking
river to forget this side?

Even there Father O'Keefe's grudging Requiem
douses the puttied flesh into
Abraham's bosom. And there boys recollect
the cortege of black limos parting

Fords to the roadside for the silent hearse.
Our absolution is days off in the hell
of forgetfulness, so we remember,
we altar boys, the luxuries of serving

the dead, the jumpseats facing backward
inside Caddies, green awnings floating
as at lawn parties, the fresh
greenbacks tucked in our fists for good work.

We did little but were young. To be the only
messengers the bereaved could afford
we spoke into our hands, our awaited Amen
flying after O'Keefe's plain Rest in Peace.

And Sundays in flannel suits, small fedoras,
we dropped into the passing basket
envelopes of change, envelopes depicting a church
of wood, our names embossed in the corners.

Only Human

So, like Father Hoffman's gruff absolution
given *sotto voce* through the wood lattice joining us,
sinner to sinner, in the confessional box,
your litany of fears boils down
to the stone at the bottom of the cauldron.

That priest kissed his purple stole good-bye,
ushering his defrocked self
out of the confessional for good.
He took one room near the hill-suckled Tiber.
Saturdays his corporate Latin forgave me,
his head bowed in a silhouette of contrition,
his last blessing: "Go. . . ."
I have him walking the Sistine
where the fingers in fresco grace eternity with clay.

What else are space and stories good for,
I wonder, and I wonder which awful ceilings
you scan tonight for human signs.
You eye one corner, and your interior monologue
runs on about a cobweb's confusion up there
as your local nebula,
your Magellanic cloud spun out by the galaxy's widow,
the sacked eggs hanging in filaments,
ready to be stars.

How about a good story?
How humans were forged into bone constellations,
and the sullen beasts, bear, crab, goat . . . ,
how without creatures the heavens hang,
a velvet curtain hiding the burning actors.
The night is stuttering on. I'm here on this side
waiting for your tale of a common ceiling,
a sky drawn over our vulgar chapel of tongues.

The Deposition

The eyes? I said the sun
inhaled them so eyesockets
held air, souvenirs of vision.

I have watched for days
as shoots of grass probed
its feathers and breastdown

for a single way to grow.
My hand has traveled words
as quickly and as ignorantly

as that grass just to say
the sun's light glinted
off the brassy backs

of two houseflies who stood,
motionless, on its left wing
while small worms crawled

through the belly's pouch.
The night throws a silk cape
over dead birds and stands guard.

Oh, a dog breaks his rounds
to stop and take a sniff,
then rolls over in its odor

and a moth, perhaps weary of air,
rests on it for ten seconds
before flying into the brightest

rip in the darkness.
Someone must dream of it.
Each morning the earth wakes

in a cool, glistening sweat
so that now, as I dare
to walk barefoot in grass

damp from that bad dream
I can see what remains.
Black feet clutching air,

a swab of down, four feathers,
the dulled beak a dark seed
and inside the cage of bones

a beetle who clicks his mandibles
once, twice, then escapes bearing
a bead of water on his back.

Trespassing on McKenzie Creek

Step easy, this farmer is rumored
to keep a double-barrel loaded
with ground glass. Remembering her
powerful dresses, he blasts holes
in fog, a pair of simple vowels.
At the kitchen table he palms
a scissored photo, the final ace.

When we imagine his creek
we trespass. May he forgive us,
two mongrels sniffing a story,
crawling under fencelines. He makes
touch dangerous, each wire
set like fine triggers, barbs
filed to teeth of fighting dogs.

This creek begins in the sky:
a man and a woman shaking dice:
one part this, one part that:
rain. No doubt he swears
he owns his blood. In a backroom
an acquaintance will drain it off
as poison. He has willed it
to the woman wearing the gift hat.

His cold creek gnaws our ankles.
Under the knotted roots
of his house, in the petrified
heart of a mammoth, the creek
is woven together. Upstream,
on the calm pool dammed up
by boulders, our faces nervously wait.

They must have walked here Sundays.
Under your eyes, going extinct,
leaves are frantic. He saw small fish
schooling the back of her head.
I cup water in my hands to drink
two faces. Notions about lovers
shimmer on the rocky creekbed.
I have trespassed. I have no sorrow.

The Fifth Season
— *for David Graham*

Waiting for the doctor (whose real name you had a hunch
was Diogenes *something* Duck)

you scanned the hieroglyphics in your palms,
also reading my dog of a mind. Like your paired hands,

my hemispheres can add up to a stunning
zero. That's why for me

each good joke is the knocking
on the night door. A knothole closes around Chaplin,

clicking his heels at The End, and just what do you think
our nervous systems do? They bare our teeth

in laughter against the wolf, huffing and puffing.
Whisper inside our stick house that nothing

tickles us, that in the atomic world
of Democritus we are the indivisible ones and the void,

our own meat and zero. Maybe Madame Hazel
will make a house call.

Maybe Hazel will tell off the universes
in the script of our fortunate palms,

in those atoms of our Crab Nebulae.
Waiting for no doctor, Bodhidharma

sat crosslegged until his hams were cured, today's lesson
in the Classic Comic entitled Patience,

a Pre-Cautionary Tale. In tomorrow's match
Fumon is pinned to his reed mat,

gazing into his own crystal of death. *Magnificent*,
he says, *Magnificent*.

No one knows the final word.
The ocean bed's aflame,

out of the void leap wooden lambs.
I don't know about you, I can't read the coffee grounds,

so what can we do but decipher
each other's scrawled mind. Like and unlike

the neurologists pulling through their clean fingers
the electroencephalograms, we ponder

one another's graph and proclaim,
We're healed! But healed of what original crime

or capital disease? Fumon's void
where the wooden

lambs gambol? A plutonic atom of Democritus
that might be nothing but a charge, or less?

We're in a fix, so we might as well throw back our faces,
show the sky our pearlies,

and laugh, for something up there is wolf to our pig,
final word to our tongue.

All I know today: snow at mind's end.
The window thermometer with the praying hands

reports fifty degrees out there, but snow conceals
the old garden where I have lain like a dog, snapping at flies.

Icicles our length are hanging
from the eaves and dripping on the wooden porch, a drumming

water clock for this fifth season,
our minds' season.

Got a minute? Then take this short walk with me
to the untrammeled snow, a radiant field,

where the scarecrow the children call Mr. Sund
lies scrawled at mind's end.

We know: he is sticks, rags, a man's old fedora.
Let's say: He's a character inked in the snow.

The Peaceable Kingdom

I hide no grenade in a hollow book,
no god in my tongue. My note is the threat
of a paper tiger: "Tell our pilot
to bank over Fond du Lac and a friend."

From here you're small in the peace of distance.
In an echoing house you read out loud
the book of divorce, and still her goddamned
red hairs materialize on your sheet.

From here a man dressed in street clothes would freeze
before he cratered the earth. I don't know
how to liberate you from your Gaza
of marriage.

          A few words and I have flown
by the bonfires of the stars, and below
the peaceable kingdom lights our way down.

FIVE

The widening

V

of its wake

The Sentence of Memory

Then, lying spread-eagle in the raked lawn
as if he had fallen from the Chinese elm,
the boy witnessed a senseless afternoon,
its general smell, his parents stirring
the heap of smoldering leaves, and leaves
curling inward, blackened, then gray.

His half-grown body took in the unnamed.
A branch overhead stirred for him to recall.
The never-ending sky pulled leafsmoke past
two down-turned faces, toward the tiny airplane
dragging its sound a handspan behind it.
The simplest bird dropped down its call.

As evidence he keeps smoke, sky, and bird,
the undeciphered world, to do justice,
naming, then naming again. His parents burn
the afternoon down. He must come up with
words to loosen their coarse-grained hands
from wooden handles, severing pity from love,

the sentence of memory. He thinks *afternoon*
until his father rubs the leafsmoke from
still good eyes. Until the simple bird grows
into nighthawk and his mother with no pain
draws off dark gloves, the three of them
cannot walk into the night the boy lets down.

The Great Bear over Grand Junction, Colorado

That summer I noted the calf's bones
turning whiter in the unadulterated sun so
coolly I could have been a second Grand Mesa
or outer space. Indifferent air worked
the russet hide away and showed the white
jail of ribs. My friend still used
whiskey to feel something, even pain,
in temples and eyes as if that stinging shot
with blood meant joy was out there.
He was fat. At our factory he worked
himself into an ignoble sweat near the plastics
oven. His name was George, that's all I
can remember. He sang Hank Williams and limericks.
Evenings we walked the irrigation canals and
sat under cottonwoods to watch dusk
lay down its silk over that spent water.
Before the breeze went up the mountains it made
leaves wave like a village bidding so long.
We drank potboilers and watched idling
mallards show how water flowed around
them to the Gulf of Baja. Once a coyote
walked past on the other bank without
sensing, and once George pointed to the Great
Bear and said, *that used to be me.*
There were two times at the canal, dusk
laying silk down flat on the water and
water always inching under it. It
must be good enough to quit the Earth
once and lie spread-eagle in the heavens
for us to get our bearings, and good enough
for bones to bleach in sunlight after
the body ends its pain, and not good
enough that summer to stay here always.

Bear Skull in the Attic

Like a balance scale I heft you bobbing in one hand.
You've lost weight on the big diet,
less now than a nursing baby, more than puppy Rex.
Still the planet pulls you down, unfinished business.

You bare long canines, untouched by the house mice,
for the last joke: prey on your own bone dust.
Rows of molars clenched as in the bad dream
of your foot in the steel trap that looks like you.
And your skull, streamlined as a bullet, races
to catch your bite, or stretches away from the sockets
as if brain, that kill-joy, lagged behind your hunger,
as if it shied away from the eye-world.

Well, what's your job in the afterlife?
Paperweight? Memento for the trashman? Garden bonemeal?
The attic looks like The Morpheus Arms Motel
for you, your family of frayed ropes finger thick,
rusting pulleys lifting no one up,
pot-bellied stove balanced on three claw feet.
The Earth at hard labor sandpapers all of you
back to iron, to cellulose, back to calcium.

Thing between a beast and Gabriel,
until the planet pulls you through the oak floors,
gaze out the attic window at carrot heads
and crab apples, at mice in the snow and rabbits.
You're omnivorous, as we are, hungry a lifetime.

Pass It On
— *for Robert Stewart*

I'm trying to piece together one river from the river-feelings
stewing on the back burner. It's like
reconstituting any old memory. Just add water, since we're mostly
water.
That acquaintance you made time with, her whole face
is in soft focus, but her ducklike ambling
remains, and her dear ignorance of it. And another thing: "the
benign."

Maybe there is just one, the way every downpour is still
the first rain, for it's always falling pitchforks
somewhere, the way each emotion is the last. This river was just
another Ozark stream on the lookout
for potential flotsam. You and I had city in graffiti
all over us, learned in the frontier thesis: put walls up
against wild innocence, erect the dwellings and christen the metropolis
Possum Trot, then hang the nude called Kitty over the bar, the Great
American Desert in the parlor, passing it on, these beauties
we sweated through, mastering.
So we weren't seduced by the Big Piney's come-hither clarity.
No, not much. And pigs fly. (Once a cabbie
whipped out pictures of "Ocelot" from his goose-down vest.
She was in mink sprawled across a Caddie's hood, and the man said,
"Man,

check it out. A hundred." Her eyes
were suckholes.) There were stones on the bottom looking up at us.
I believe we paddled over them, believe
we canoed on into our charted fears and the real rush
we had driven miles to inherit, adrenaline
doing its job, the mapped boulders at their stations.
And it felt good.

                What's left of anything
but hard-boiled eggs pickled in jars, the cool mind housing
the old hot facts. I think there is a world out there,
and a woman nursing a beer at the Do Drop Inn.
She's not Mother Nature, this beast of beauty, not anymore.

Lost Landscape

From this asphalt road cracked by milk trucks
you could gaze west, as a friend and I just did,

discovering a lost landscape with two figures,
a lost Millet. In it you could catch sight of two farmers,

one leaning on a wooden rake watching the other,
and the other raking the sweet hay into a row and shade.

On this road you may as well put out of mind
pretty stories that landscapes tell,

the picture offering two haystacks as huts for the gleaners,
or the one giving the horizon a gray smudge for a steeple,

its toll for the Angelus muffled.
If you stand closer to this electric fence

two farmers will age before you.
What you saw as a crosshatched brow will grow to wrinkles,

the dark you mistook for a shaded cheek
maturing to dirt, fists blotched and rough as potatoes

materializing as hands.
The fence running silent with its current around them

marks the land where your eyes fail
to see those two are brothers.

My friend and I can tell you the one raking is Alvyn,
his left eye askew ten degrees

so he sees even you doubled.
A drab workshirt threadbare at the elbows

is his uniform this week. What does Sunday mean?
A white shirt, a black bow his brother Tom helps him tie.

From the electric fence
you can't see Tom's teeth are gone,

that he wears the aroma of their milking barn
seventy years like a robe.

Gazing farther west to the maples
you will not see the figure in gray, the stiff

field boss astride his black horse,
the foreman who for years has egged those two on

to the salt of sweat, to the itch of hay
down the ravines of their backs,

to beds growing their shapes for six decades.
Catching sight of two farmers can free

them to another land, one held down by stones
that Grandfather Barrus stacked up one spring in the shape

of a man, and by a sky
all gray, cracking under the weight.

Third Island

Locals call it Third Island, that entity of scrub and silt
at odds with the river, keeping oval, unriver.

Imagine this is our next life: walking hunched into
a perpetual North wind, how we would grow in awe of our feet.
Think of work, its duty to shape us,
you lard ass, you hunk,

my raving beauty, you egghead. In or on *National Geographic*
don't flooding rivers "carve islands"
out of the bottomlands, so the bottomlands
hold some secret islands, so the river islands
didn't just revolt, secede, set up their dominions?

We can film this on Third Island, a dozen picnickers rising
from blankets, dusting their hands off
in that way that says, "We're ready, let's measure the island."
They hold hands, a human net across the width of the island.
And the Labrador retriever, his nose discovering
nothing promising for his hunger, paddles home. . . .

When snow meets the river, bodies go back to water,
short crystalline life, long fluid one.
Third Island grows abstract, "like the framework
of my dream home, my iceberg home,"
at least that's what the schoolkid thinks crossing the bridge,
throwing slushballs at the river. So many of us
watch Third Island, from the corners of our eyes
traveling River Road, or head-on from second floor bedrooms,
triangulating our daily movements, so that when the island's
whiteness falls off and the brown bleeds through
and the river, flooding, leaves only branches above flood stage,

we feel culpable, our merely keeping watch
an act of our larger will.
If that's the plot, are we the agents for Spring,
the green wedding on Third Island, are we photosynthesis?

Soon a blue tent and mystery
will summer on Third Island and we on the riverbanks
will hear that guest, our ears to the temperate breezes, singing
in his night tongue as he nightfishes
though to him we are beyond the dead air of the crevasse.

— *in memory of W. S. Graham*

Triptych: A Joyful Noise
— *for Kelly McFarland*

1. The Left Panel

There's a quick blow, her shoulder goes numb, and
pain starts its radiation, all bringing
news that her fiance ponders his hand,

a cinder block overhead, her asking
herself, "Where's the rest of the concrete wall?"

the cinder block coming down on her head,
the stupid thing drooping to her hands, all
her scalp now like glass that being shattered
is given feeling,

                the old messenger
inside of her, — talking hands? a charged space? —
informing her: "He is killing you. Hide."

"No," shoes say, the kitchen is kicking her,
crouched under the kitchen table, her face
under remembered sheets where she once hid.

2. The Darker Head Remembering Alive inside Her

It was dark for a while, and got darker.
Sitting up in bed later with a shaved head
she drank through straws, almost remembering
being unconscious, — "like posing inside
a statue made of coal that comes alive."
It was dark, and the statue mothered her.

Coming back to life meant welcoming her
own prodigal pain, meant that the darker
mother adopting her was burned alive
as a statue of coal. Her white, wrapped head
was a balloon filled with water inside.
Her lips swelled, as if remembering

plum lipstick and eyelids, remembering
how they told him things, and things he told her.
Now her lips were violet, and inside
the incisors missing, her mouth darker.
The sutures did not itch yet in her head.
She drank through a bent straw, and felt alive.

Healing was a kind of chant, cells alive
a capella in her flesh remembering
when love was love, and the joyful noise ahead.
And the charged space between cells forgave her
as a victim, her hair grew in darker
and new scars had the sheen of silk. Inside

was a room arranging itself. Inside
the room a crouched figure, dead or alive?
She would paint this, with all of the darker
strokes outside the picture, remembering.

It would look like a pastel X-ray, of her!
The theme? Hope. A painting was in her head:

a picture that balances on the head
of the crouched figure, floorless as if inside
an autumnal cloudscape, three chairs near her
colored in cream or bone, the most alive
things (looking right out, as though remembering),
a table, two cinder blocks over a darker

head, charcoal eyes asking, "Am I alive?"
Inside a painting floats, remembering
her in a painting, no longer darker.

3. Life in the Jet Stream

This morning, inhabited by you, like I was your personal hideaway,
I walked out and leaned against a warm, parked car,
kind of embracing it. A pleasure it was to rest
my arms on the roof, then my chin on my hands,
and my back to the sun, diffused through the green gauze of May.
I evicted you for a moment. Forgive me.

Up there, the jet stream was ushering
the air liners (and I half-prayed that the passengers
would come back life-size after landing) eastward
toward some islands where our ancestors noisily boarded ships,
their heavy shoes drumming the gangway
despite their holding their breaths.

                                      And here we are,
exhaling but scarred, and joyous despite everything, —
hell, joyous *due* to everything! —
and the jet stream is bringing a parade of . . .
colored ribbons, the ribs of fish, wavy sand on a beach,
the heads of Presidents, creatures
from the sky's bestiary, spheres, Biblical cities, and domes,
all made out of cirrus, stratocumulus, and contrails,
our breaths, cosmic dust, dirt.

What do they do up there?
"You tell me."

*   *   *

They are all seated and comfy, facing east
as though watching old Hollywood movies,
but there are no movies, just the wind forever
at their backs like a beatitude fulfilled

Or they're like those pictures on the walls of pyramids,
people in profile with skin like clay
and wigs glistening with scented fat, going
to weigh their hearts against the feather of truth

Only life in the jet stream has no balance scale,
and they are translucent, slightly pink, like wax candy people
emptied of their sweet, sticky fluid,
and we know how we devoured that juice, don't we?

Oh, they are civil to one another
(the jet stream is *nothing* if not a civilized construct, —
sonnets, summer dachas, Zeus in feathers —)
offering one another magazines, or drinks freshened

But sometimes we do hear them, catching
on T.V. antennas or favorite trees,
or on monuments like the Arch near where you call home,
a sound like old, muffled sirens, but they feel no pain

They just remember May, luxurious green again
that outlasts them, the telling stories and pictures
going on inside the lengthening grass,
and humans beaten who can go on to praise anything.

THE JUNIPER PRIZE

This volume is the sixteenth recipient
of the Juniper Prize
presented annually by the
University of Massachusetts Press
for a volume of original poetry.
The prize is named in honor of
Robert Francis (1901-87),
who lived for many years at
Fort Juniper, Amherst, Massachusetts.